KU-165-303

Tweenies™

I'll Huff and I'll Puff!

Milo was playing
with some little sticks.
"Oh bother!" he said.
Judy came to ask him
what he was doing.
"I'm trying to build a
little house with
these sticks, but they
keep falling down."

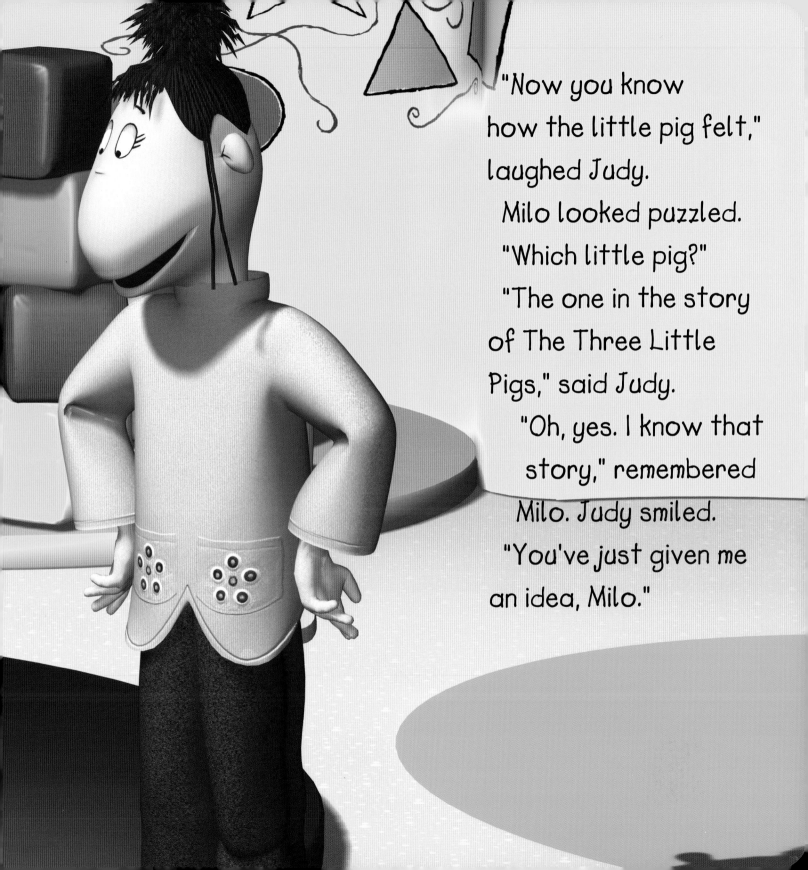

"Now you know how the little pig felt," laughed Judy.

Milo looked puzzled.

"Which little pig?"

"The one in the story of The Three Little Pigs," said Judy.

"Oh, yes. I know that story," remembered Milo. Judy smiled.

"You've just given me an idea, Milo."

Judy called the others.

"How about acting out the story of The Three Little Pigs?" she asked. The Tweenies cheered.

Judy showed them how they could build a house out of the squishy shapes and then she found two big pieces of paper.

"On one, we'll stick Milo's twigs and on the other we'll stick some straw. Then we can use sticky tape to stick them on the front of the house, depending on which part of the story we've got to," she said.

So Bella and Milo built the house while Fizz and Jake started the sticking.

The scenery was soon ready – and so were the Tweenies!
"I'd like to be the pig who makes his house out of
sticks," said Milo.
"And can I be the pig whose house is
made of straw?" asked Fizz.

Bella looked glum.

"I don't really want to be a pig or a wolf," she said.

"Why don't you tell the story, Bella," said Judy. "Jake can be the pig who makes a house with bricks, and Doodles can be the Big Bad Wolf."

So Judy and Izzles settled down to watch and the play began.

"Once upon a time," said Bella, "there were three little pigs who each decided to build a house."

"We know a song about building a house," Fizz interrupted. "Let's sing it now!"

Fizz, Milo and Jake
began to sing.

I'm going to build a house,
With a chimney tall,
A sloping roof,
And a garden wall.

A big front door you can open wide,
And two tiny windows you can peep inside.
I'm going to build a house,
I'm going to build a house.

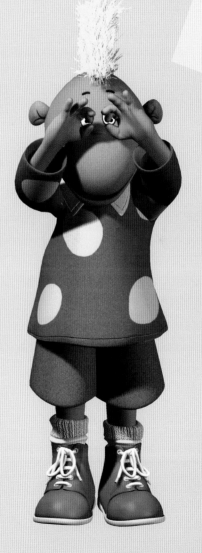

I'm going to build a table,
Big enough for two,
Two little chairs,
One for me and one for you.

Knock on the door and please come in,
My house is shining like a bright new pin.
I'm going to build a house,
I'm going to build a house.

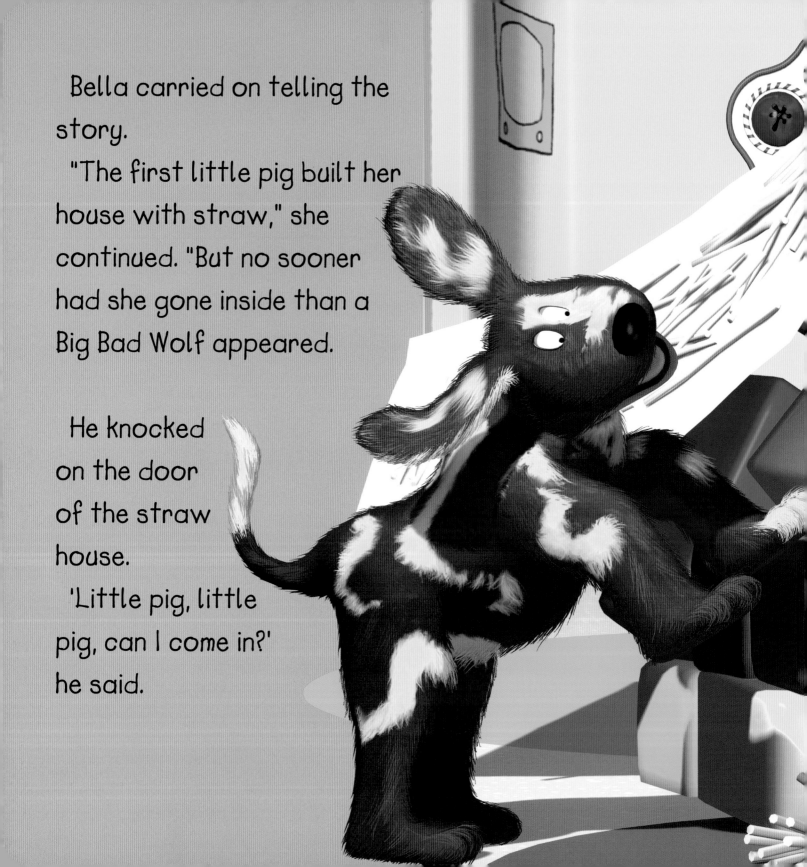

Bella carried on telling the story.

"The first little pig built her house with straw," she continued. "But no sooner had she gone inside than a Big Bad Wolf appeared.

He knocked on the door of the straw house.

'Little pig, little pig, can I come in?' he said.

The first little pig looked out of the window, saw the wolf and said,

'No, no! By the hair of my chinny chin-chin, I shall not let you in!

'All right, I'll huff and I'll puff and I'll blow your house down,' said the wolf.

So he huffed and he puffed and blew the straw house down. The first little pig squealed and ran to find the second little pig.

The second little pig had built his house with sticks. And when he heard the first little pig's story he quickly let her in.

No sooner were they inside than the Big Bad Wolf appeared and he knocked on the door.

'Little pigs, little pigs, can I come in?' he said.
The second little pig looked out of the window and said,

'No, no! By the hair of my chinny chin-chin, I shall not let you in!'

'All right, I'll huff and I'll puff and I'll blow your house down,' said the wolf.

So he huffed and he puffed and blew the stick house down. The two little pigs screeched and ran to find the third little pig.

The third little pig had built his house with bricks. And when he heard about the wolf, he let the others in.

No sooner were they inside than the Big Bad Wolf appeared and knocked on the door of the brick house.

'Little pigs, little pigs, can I come in?' The third little pig looked out of the window and said,

'No, no! By the hair of my chinny chin-chin, I shall not let you in!'

'All right, I'll huff and I'll puff and I'll blow your house down,' said the wolf.

So he huffed and he puffed and blew ... but nothing happened. So he huffed and he puffed and he blew some more ... and still nothing happened.

The wolf couldn't understand why the house wouldn't fall down and he tried again. He huffed and he puffed, and he huffed and he puffed, and he huffed and he fell over from all the huffing and puffing.

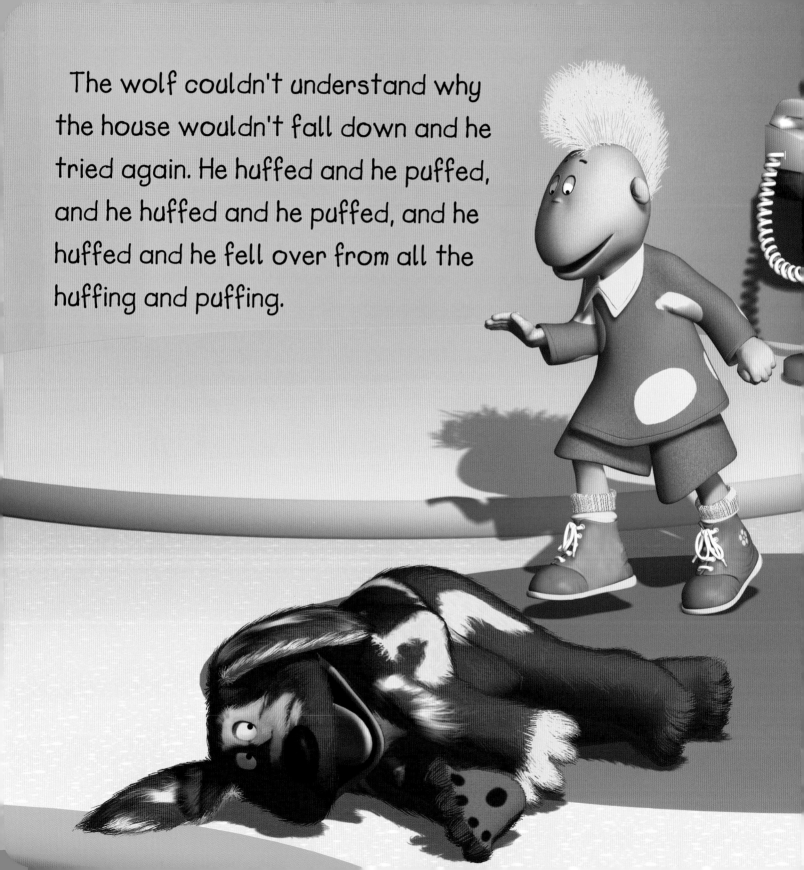

Meanwhile, the little pigs sneaked out
of the brick house. They crept up behind
the wolf and shouted...

BOO!

The wolf got such a fright he leapt into the air and ran and ran and ran and was never seen again.

'Thank you for letting us hide in your house,' said the second little pig.

'You were very sensible to build it with bricks!' said the first little pig.

And the little pigs decided to move into the brick house where they all lived happily ever after."

Then Jake noticed that Doodles was missing.

They found him in the playhouse. He really had been
frightened when the Tweenies shouted 'BOO!'.
"Sorry, Doodles!" said Milo. "It was only a joke."

Izzles came running in. She was looking for the Tweenies and Doodles.

She ran...

...right into the house of bricks!

"Oh dear!" laughed Jake. "My house of bricks wasn't so strong after all!"

And everyone else laughed, too.

THE END